The VOICE of the GREAT BELL

by LAFCADIO HEARN
retold by
MARGARET HODGES
illustrated by
ED YOUNG

Little, Brown and Company • Boston • Toronto • London

The Voice of the Great Bell is retold by Margaret Hodges from the story
"The Soul of the Great Bell" by Lafcadio Hearn, first published in 1887
in his collection of stories entitled *Some Chinese Ghosts*
(Boston: Roberts Brothers).

"The Voice of the Great Bell" by Margaret Hodges appeared previously in
Tell It Again: Great Tales from Around the World (Dial, 1963).

Library of Congress Cataloging-in-Publication Data

Hodges, Margaret.
   The voice of the great bell / by Lafcadio Hearn; retold by
Margaret Hodges; illustrated by Ed Young. — 1st ed.
      p.   cm.
   "Retold . . . from the story 'The soul of the great bell' by
Lafcadio Hearn" — T.p. verso.
   Summary: A Chinese bell-maker's daughter makes a noble sacrifice
so that the casting of The Great Bell for the emperor will be
flawless.
   ISBN 0-316-36791-5:
   [1. Folklore — China.] I. Young, Ed. ill. II. Hearn, Lafcadio,
1850–1904. Soul of the great bell. III. Title.
PZ8.1.H69Vo 1989
398.2'0951 — dc19
[E]   88-15389
                                                                         CIP
                                                                          AC

10 9 8 7 6 5 4 3 2 1

NIL

Published simultaneously in Canada
by Little, Brown & Company (Canada) Limited

Printed in Italy

Illustrations done in pastel and watercolor on Stonehenge acid-free paper.
Color separations made by New Interlitho.
Text set in Palatino by Litho Composition Company, Inc.
Display lines done in calligraphy by Jeanne Wong.
Printed and bound by New Interlitho, Milan, Italy.

For Toki Koizumi, whose grandfather, Lafcadio Hearn,
gave this story to East and West

M. H.

To Liu Hsi Hung, my elder brother,
for his teaching and inspiration

E. Y.

Hear the great bell! Ko-Ngai! Ko-Ngai! All the little dragons on the high-tilted eaves of the green roofs shiver to the tips of their gilded tails under that deep wave of sound. All the hundred little bells of the pagodas quiver with desire to speak. Ko-Ngai! Even so the great bell has sounded every day for five hundred years — Ko-Ngai! First with stupendous clang of brass, then with a golden tone, then with silver murmuring. Now, this is the story of the great bell.

Nearly five hundred years ago the Emperor of China, Son of Heaven, commanded a worthy man, Kouan-Yu, to have a bell made so big that the sound might be heard for a hundred miles. The voice of the bell should be strengthened with brass and deepened with gold and sweetened with silver, all added to the cast iron, and the bell should be hung in the center of the Chinese capital to sound through all the many-colored ways of the City of Peking.

Kouan-Yu assembled
the most famous bellmakers of
the empire, and they measured the
materials and prepared the molds,
the fires, the instruments, and the mon-
strous melting pot for fusing the metal. And
they labored like giants, neglecting rest and
sleep and the comforts of life, toiling both night
and day in obedience to Kouan-Yu, and striving
in all things to do the will of the Son of Heaven.

When the metal had melted into a glowing mass of
liquid, it was poured into the mold. And when it had
cooled, the earthen mold was broken away. Then it was
discovered that in spite of their great labor and ceaseless
care, the metals fell apart. The gold would not blend with the
brass, the silver would not mingle with the molten iron.

Once more the molds had to be prepared, and the fires re-
kindled, and the metal remelted, and all the tiresome, hard work
repeated. The Son of Heaven heard and was angry, but said nothing.

A second time the bell was cast, and the result was even worse. Still the metals refused to blend one with the other, and the sides of the bell were cracked and its lips were broken away, so that all the labor had to be repeated even a third time, to the great dismay of Kouan-Yu. And when the Son of Heaven heard these things, he was angrier than before, and he sent his messenger to Kouan-Yu with a letter written upon lemon-colored silk and sealed with the Seal of the Dragon, saying:

"Twice hast thou betrayed the trust we have placed in thee. If thou fail a third time in fulfilling our command, thou shalt die. Tremble and obey!"

Now, Kouan-Yu had a daughter of dazzling loveliness. Her name was Ko-Ngai, and her heart was even more beautiful than her face. Ko-Ngai loved her father so much that she had refused a hundred offers of marriage rather than leave him lonely, and when she had seen the Emperor's letter, sealed with the Dragon Seal, she feared for her father's sake. She could not rest or sleep for thinking of his danger.

Secretly, she sold some of her jewels, and with the money she went to an astrologer and paid him a great price to tell her how she might save her father from the danger that hung over him.

The astrologer looked at the stars, marked the position of the Milky Way, examined the signs of the Zodiac, and consulted the mystical books of the magicians. After a long silence he answered her, saying:

"Gold and brass will never join one with the other, silver and iron will never embrace until a pure maiden is melted with them in the crucible."

So Ko-Ngai returned home sorrowful at heart, but she kept secret all that she had heard and told no one what she had done.

At last came the awful day for the third and last effort to cast the great bell. Ko-Ngai, accompanied by her servant, went with her father to the foundry. They took their places upon a platform overlooking the working molders and the lava of molten metal.

All the workmen toiled in silence. No sound was heard but the muttering of the fire. And the muttering deepened into a roar like the roar of great waves, and the blood red lake of metal slowly brightened like a crimson sunrise, and the crimson became a radiant glow of gold, and the gold turned to a blinding white, like the silver face of a full moon.

Then the workmen stopped feeding the hungry flame and all fixed their eyes upon the eyes of Kouan-Yu. Kouan-Yu prepared to give the signal to pour the metal into the mold.

But before he could lift his finger, a cry caused him to turn his head. And all heard the voice of Ko-Ngai, sounding sharply sweet as a bird's song above the great thunder of the fires — "For thy sake, O my father!"

And even as she cried, she leapt into the white flood of metal, and the lava of the furnace roared to receive her. Flakes of flame spattered to the roof and burst over the edge of the earthen crater and cast up a whirling fountain of many-colored fires.

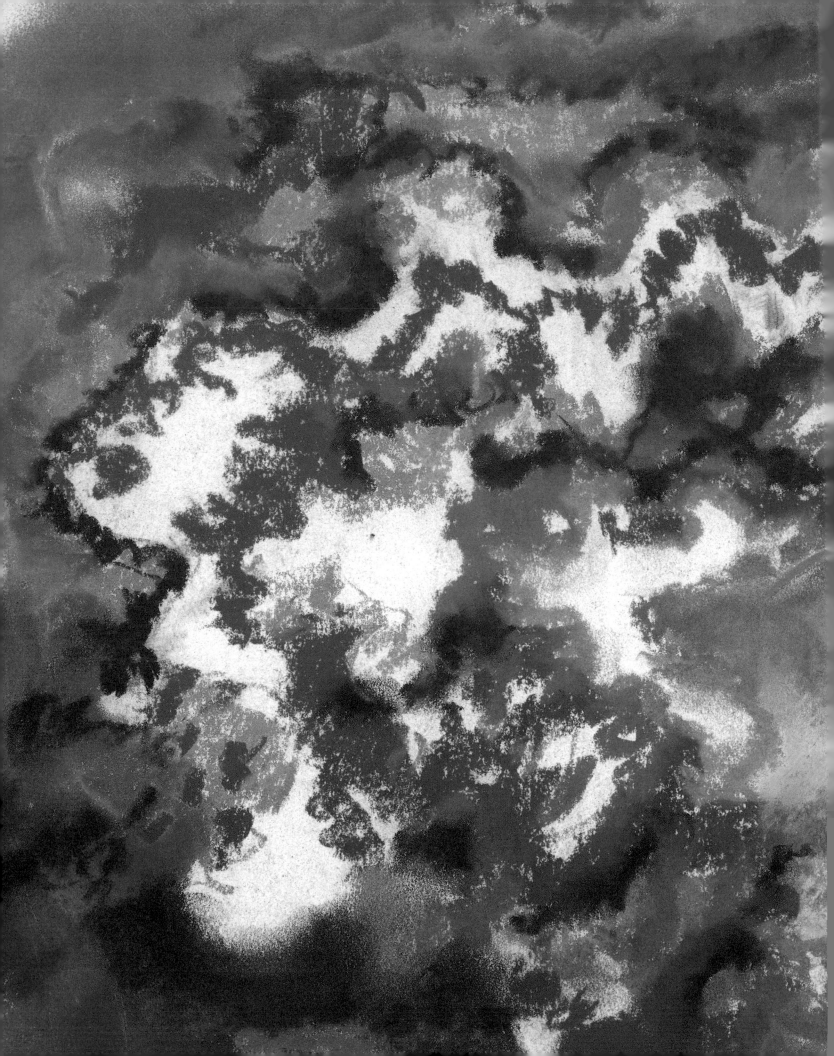

Then the fire died down, with lightnings and with thunders and with mutterings. Wild with grief, the father of Ko-Ngai would have leapt in after her. But strong men held him back and kept a firm grasp upon him until they could carry him home.

And the servant of Ko-Ngai, dizzy and speechless, stood before the furnace, still holding in her hand a shoe, a tiny, dainty shoe, with embroidery of pearls and flowers — the shoe of her beautiful mistress. For she had tried to grasp Ko-Ngai by the foot as she leapt, but she had only been able to clutch the shoe, and the pretty shoe came off in her hand.

In spite of all these things, the command of the Emperor had to be obeyed and the work finished, hopeless as the result might be. Yet the glow of the metal seemed purer and whiter than before. So the heavy casting was made.

And lo! When the metal had become cool, it was found that the bell was beautiful to look upon, and perfect in form, and wonderful in color above all other bells.

Of Ko-Ngai herself no trace was left. She had become part of
the bell, blended with the well-blended brass and gold, with the
mingled silver and iron. And when they sounded the bell, its tones
were found to be deeper and mellower and mightier than the tones
of any other bell, like a pealing of summer thunder, yet also like some
vast voice uttering a name, a girl's name — the name of Ko-Ngai!

And still when Chinese mothers hear the voice of the great bell in all the many-colored ways of Peking, they whisper to their little ones: "Listen! That is Ko-Ngai crying for her shoe! That is Ko-Ngai calling for her shoe!"

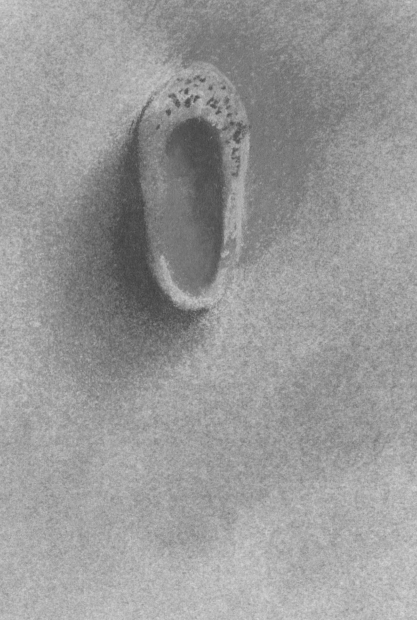